CW00859089

Big Bad Chief Lino

By L. Michelle Tago-Tu'itupou

Illustrated by Ash Grover

Copyright © 2019 L. Michelle Tago-Tu'itupou
All rights reserved.

No part of this publication may be reproduced, distributed, or transmitted in any form or by any means, or stored in a database or retrieval system, without the prior written permission of the author.

All characters and events in this publication, other than those clearly in the public domain, are fictitious. Any similarity to real persons, living or dead, is coincidental and not intended by the author. The author does not claim to be an expert in Pasifika culture and has taken artistic liberties in telling the story.

Cover design and illustrations by Ash Grover

Copyright © 2019 L. Michelle Tago-Tu'itupou
All rights reserved.
ISBN: 9781708713737

DEDICATION
For my brother, Lino
April 3, 1973 - August 20, 2006
The fat lady sang WAY too soon. We love
and miss you every single day.

ACKNOWLEDGMENTS

For all the past, present, and future Pasifika story tellers. Let our voices be heard.

E sau le fuata ma lona lou.
In every generation there are some outstanding chiefs.

On a small island in the South Pacific there were four sisters. They lived with their parents in a fale by the sea. The oldest sister was very tall and skinny with frizzy hair. She couldn't see very well so she was always squinting her eyes. As the oldest, she was very bossy. Her full name meant "lei of life" but her family called her Kalei.

The second sister loved to play sports. She was always hot, so she liked her hair short. She liked talking and arguing with her sisters. She was also very good with numbers. Her full name meant "fragrant breeze" but her family called her Moani.

The third sister was small and skinny so that helped her be the sneakiest sneak in the world. She was very quiet and liked to be alone. She also loved to draw pictures of flowers and trees. Her name meant "the flower" but her family called her Pua.

The fourth and youngest sister was very young, and she was just learning how to speak. She loved music. She was always singing or dancing. She also had a very soft heart and would cry when people felt sad. Her full name meant "adored one" but her family called her Nana.

All four sisters had beautiful brown hair, dark brown eyes, and were very smart. They did everything together since there were no other people nearby. Or so they thought.

One warm summer morning, the girls woke up to find their parents were very sick. So sick, in fact, they couldn't get out of bed. The girls' dad couldn't go fishing and their mom couldn't get food from the garden. She was too sick to even cook!

The four sisters were very scared and very hungry. Since they were too young to start the cooking fires and everything in the garden had to be cooked, the girls decided to walk to their ma'umaga to pick some fruit from the trees.

"Should we leave Nana at home with mama and papa?" Moani asked.

"No," Kalei responded immediately. "I don't want her wandering off to the ocean. You know how she loves to swim. Plus, we should all stay together. It's safer that way."

"Can I stay home?" Pua asked. She hated going places.

Kalei glared at her and replied sharply, "No! We stay together."

They made sure their parents had water and were comfortable. With heavy sighs, the four sisters began their journey to get some food at their family's ma'umaga.

Moani talked while the other sisters stayed quiet. She talked about how she threw a rock from their house and almost reached the ocean. She talked about climbing the coconut tree until their mother caught her and yelled for her to get down before she fell. She talked and talked.

About halfway to the ma'umaga, the girls passed by a giant boulder. Beyond the boulder there was an overgrown pathway that led to a rundown fale in the distance.

Kalei shushed Moani as the girls stopped to look at this unusual sight. They thought their nearest neighbors were at least a one day walk from their home. Curious, they stood in front of the boulder wondering who used to live there.

Suddenly, the boulder began to move.

Kalei squinted her eyes and asked, "What's happening?"

"The boulder is moving," said Moani, who looked scared, but ready for a fight.

"Let's run and hide," said Pua, who always wanted to be sneaky.

Nana stared and said nothing. She held Kalei's hand tightly.

It was too late to do anything. The boulder stopped moving and a large man jumped out in front of the girls.

"Who are you and what do you want?" the large man asked loudly.

"We're not supposed to talk to strangers," Moani answered boldly.

"Yeah," said Pua. "So leave us alone."

Nana tugged on Kalei's arm. "Bad man?" she asked quietly.

"Wait," Kalei paused, thinking for a minute.

"Mama used to tell me about the big man who lived in the fale near our ma'umaga. She said he was very mean and always yelled at the kids. I thought she said he moved away a long time ago. She also said he was 'aiga. He's family. You must be Big Bad Chief Lino!"

"That is me!" said the huge man. "And yes, I moved away for a long time, but now I have returned. What are you four young girls doing walking all alone? Where are your parents?"

Kalei looked sadly at the chief and Moani's eyes began to water. Pua and Nana began to cry.

"Please, Big Bad Chief Lino!" Pua sobbed. "Our mom and dad are very sick and the only food we can get to eat is at our ma'umaga!"

The chief looked thoughtfully at the four sisters and asked, "What are you getting to eat?"

The girls replied quietly, "Guava."

"I will let you pass by my fale if you promise to share some of your guava with me," said Big Bad Chief Lino.

"Oh, thank you," the girls answered. "We promise we'll share our guava."

The girls walked the rest of the way to their ma'umaga, picked as many guava as they could carry, dropped some off with Big Bad Chief Lino, and went home.

The next day the girls' mom and dad were still very sick, and they had eaten all their guava. Their parents couldn't eat anything, so they made sure they had enough water to drink.

"What are we going to do?" Pua asked.

"I scared of mean man," Nana said softly.

Moani looked worried. "We have to go back to the ma'umaga for food, but that means passing by…"

"Big Bad Chief Lino," the three older girls said at the same time.

Being the oldest, Kalei made the final decision.

"We have no other choice. We need food and the only food we can get is at the ma'umaga."

Moani looked like she was going to argue. The look on Kalei's face made her stop. The girls began their second journey to the ma'umaga keeping their eyes open for Big Bad Chief Lino.

As they passed by the boulder, the girls held their breath. Just when they thought they were safely past, Big Bad Chief Lino jumped out in front of them.

"Aue!" screamed the sisters.

"You four again!" yelled Big Bad Chief Lino. "What are you doing here alone?"

The girls stared at the chief with wide eyes. Finally, Kalei whispered, "Our parents are still sick, and we need more food."

"Still sick?" Big Bad Chief Lino said in a stern voice.

"Well, what are you getting from your ma'umaga today?"

Moani gulped and said, "Mangoes."

Big Bad Chief Lino gave the girls a stern look and then he sighed. "If you girls promise to share your mangoes with me, I will let you pass."

"We promise," the girls replied.

Kalei, Moani, Pua, and Nana walked the rest of the way to the ma'umaga, picked as many mangoes as they could carry, dropped some off with Big Bad Chief Lino, and went home.

The next day the girls' mom and dad were still very sick. They gave their parents water to drink and covered their foreheads with ti leaves. That morning, the girls had eaten the last of their mangoes for breakfast.

The four sisters stood in front of their fale staring at the road leading to their ma'umaga.

"We need more food," Pua said.

"Yup," Kalei answered.

"We'll have to get past Big Bad Chief Lino," Moani said.

"Yup," Kalei answered.

"Mean man again?" Nana asked, lip quivering.

"Yup," Kalei answered, patting her head softly.

"There's no way to sneak past him?" Pua whispered.

"Nope." Kalei let out a deep sigh and said, "Let's get this over with."

The sisters began walking to their ma'umaga, their footsteps getting heavier and heavier as they got closer to the boulder. They were almost past the boulder and almost feeling safe when the boulder began to move. Before the girls could run, Big Bad Chief Lino jumped out in front of them.

The chief looked surprised to see the girls.

"Why are you here again?" he yelled. "It's not safe for you girls to be out alone!"

The sisters stood frozen, staring at the chief with huge eyes. They were all crying. Big Bad Chief Lino sighed and scratched his head.

"Are your parents still sick?" he asked.

Kalei, Moani, Pua, and Nana just nodded their heads.

"Are you going to get more food?" the chief asked.

The girls nodded again, too afraid to speak.

In a nicer voice, Big Bad Chief Lino told the sisters, "If you promise to share your food with me, I will let you pass. What are you getting today?"

"Bananas," Pua answered in a shaky voice.

"Okay, off you go," the chief commanded, but not as stern as before.

The four sisters walked the rest of the way to their ma'umaga, picked as many bananas as they could carry, dropped some off with Big Bad Chief Lino, and went home.

The next day the girls woke up to find their parents feeling much better. Kalei, Moani, Pua, and Nana spent the morning helping their mom get food from the garden and watching their dad fish in the sea.

After a late lunch of fish, taro, and palusami, the girls sat in front of their fale feeling warm and happy.

"I'm glad mama and papa are better," Moani said.

Pua looked at her and smiled.

"Me, too," she replied.

But Kalei just stared at the road leading to their ma'umaga.

"I wonder if Big Bad Chief Lino has any food," Kalei said quietly.

The girls didn't hear their mom and Nana walk up behind them.

"Did you want to take him some?" their mom asked. She had a basket in her hand and a smile on her face.

"For mean man," Nana giggled, holding onto her mother's free hand.

"Are you going with us?" Kalei asked looking worried.

"Yes," their mom answered.

Kalei, Moani, Pua, Nana, and their mom walked down the road toward Big Bad Chief Lino's fale. When they came to the boulder, they saw a little girl sitting by the road. As soon as she saw them, she jumped up and came running.

"You need to come with me to the fale," the little girl cried.

Kalei asked, "Who are you?"

The little girl looked at them with tears in her eyes.

"I am Big Bad Chief Lino's niece, Aperila," she answered.

The girls looked surprised because they didn't know the chief had a niece! They followed Aperila into the fale.

Big Bad Chief Lino was lying on a mat with his eyes closed.

"Uncle," Aperila whispered. "The four sisters are here."

Without opening his eyes, the chief asked, "Are they alone?"

"No," Aperila answered. "Their mom is with them."

Big Bad Chief Lino smiled and opened his eyes. He looked at the girls and their mom.

"What's wrong?" Pua asked.

"I am very sick," the chief said softly.

"Are you going to get better?" Moani asked.

The chief looked sad and shook his head.

"We brought you some food," Kalei said with tears in her eyes.

Nana took the chief's hand in her own. "No more mean man?" she asked.

Big Bad Chief Lino smiled, looked at Aperila, then looked back at the sisters.

"I'm glad you came to see me," the chief said. "I wanted to give you girls a gift because you always shared your food with me. I am giving this to you, so you will stay close to home. When you wake up tomorrow morning, you will have your gift."

The girls said a tearful goodbye to Big Bad Chief Lino and Aperila. They walked home with their mom and went to sleep that night feeling very sad.

The next morning, the girls' mom and dad woke them up and said, "Come and look."

They all went outside and behind their garden was the most amazing sight. There were rows and rows of guava trees, mango trees, and banana trees, as far as the eye could see!

"This is the chief's gift," the girls' dad said. "He wanted to make sure the four of you would always have food close by and that you would always be safe."

Kalei, Moani, Pua, and Nana, with tears in their eyes, whispered, "Thank you, Big Bad Chief Lino."

Samoan Words & Pronunciation Guide

'**Aue** (ow eh): An expression that can mean "oh my"

Fale (fah leh): Samoan home that is an open structure with poles and a thatched roof either circular or oval in shape. Coconut fronds weaved together also create blinds that can be tied up in between the poles or pulled down to protect the inside from rain or wind.

Ma'umaga (mah ooh mah nga): plantation (The letter 'g' in the Samoan language is pronounced like the 'ng' in 'sing')

Kalei (kah lay)
Moani (moh ah nee)
Pua (poo ah)
Nana (nah nah)
Lino (lee noh)
Aperila (ah peh ree lah)

(Author's note: I made up this story when my three older daughters were very young as a bedtime story. The name of the chief was changed to Lino after my brother passed away. He was the stern uncle who was actually a giant teddy bear. He loved and cared for his nieces and nephews. We miss him dearly.)

ABOUT THE AUTHOR

Michelle was born and raised in American Samoa in the village of Nu'uuli to a Samoan dad and a Palagi (Caucasian) mom. As the middle child of five siblings, she loved to lose herself in books. While eating lots of chocolate. She passed on her love for reading and story telling (and chocolate!) to her four daughters. She plans to continue writing in this genre so that Pasifika children around the world can see themselves in stories written for and about them by someone who is "them." Michelle currently lives in Salt Lake City, Utah with her husband, four daughters, and two dogs, dreaming of returning to the ocean to feel the sand between her toes.

Email: michelletagotuitupou@gmail.com
Facebook: www.facebook.com/polynesianstories
Blog: www.polynesianstories.blogspot.com

Printed in Great Britain
by Amazon

33592101R00020